cornbread & poppy

matthew cordell

Little, Brown and Company
New York Boston

To Julie—
the Poppy to my Cornbread

About This Book

The illustrations for this book were done in pen and ink with watercolor. This book was edited by Mary-Kate Gaudet and designed by Lynn El-Roeiy. The series is designed by Joann Hill. The production was supervised by Kimberly Stella, and the production editor was Marisa Finkelstein. The text was set in New Century Schoolbook, and the display type is hand lettered.

 • Little, Brown and Company • Hachette Book Group • 1290 Avenue of the Americas, New York, NY 10104 • Visit us at LBYR.com • First Edition: January 2022 • Little, Brown and Company is a division of Hachette Book Group, Inc. • The Little, Brown name and logo are trademarks of Hachette Book Group, Inc. • The publisher is not responsible for websites (or their content) that are not owned by the publisher. • Library of Congress Cataloging-in-Publication Data • Names: Cordell, Matthew, 1975– author, illustrator. • Title: Cornbread & Poppy / by Matthew Cordell. • Other titles: Cornbread and Poppy • Description: First edition. | New York : Little, Brown and Company, 2022. | Series: Cornbread & Poppy; [1] | Audience: Ages 4–8. | Summary: Cautious Cornbread and carefree Poppy are best friends, so when Poppy fails to prepare for winter, Cornbread ventures up Holler Mountain with her to help her find food. • Identifiers: LCCN 2021019238 | ISBN 9780759554870 (hardcover) | ISBN 9780759554863 (paperback) | ISBN 9780759554849 (ebook) • Subjects: CYAC: Mice—Fiction. | Best friends—Fiction. | Friendship—Fiction. • Classification: LCC PZ7.C815343 Co 2022 | DDC [E]—dc23 • LC record available at https://lccn.loc.gov/2021019238 • ISBNs: 978-0-7595-5487-0 (hardcover), 978-0-7595-5486-3 (pbk.), 978-0-7595-5484-9 (ebook), 978-0-316-39923-4 (ebook), 978-0-316-39933-3 (ebook) • PRINTED IN CHINA • APS • Hardcover: 10 9 8 7 6 5 4 3 2 1 • Paperback: 10 9 8 7 6 5 4 3 2 1

5

Every autumn,
Cornbread worried
he would not have
enough food to get
through winter.

Twist!

But he also loved to
plan and prepare.

It took a lot of
planning to get
through those long,
cold winter months.

Cornbread's best friend, Poppy,
was not one to worry.

She loved adventure.

She loved to ride bikes.

She loved to take hikes. And she loved to play
on the swing set with Cornbread at her house.

But she did not love to plan or prepare. She did not love to forage.

She always put it off till the very last minute. And she was almost out of food.

BOOM! BOOM! There was a knock at Cornbread's door.

"Time to forage for winter!" yelled Poppy.

"Poppy!" said Cornbread, "It *is* winter! You didn't get your food? Surely, it's all gone by now!"

"What do you mean, 'all gone'?"

13

"Don't you remember," asked Cornbread,
"when I asked you to come with me to get your
cheese from Sam's Dairy?

"'He's almost out,'
I said. And what
did you say?"

"But I was riding my
bike!" Poppy said.

"Don't you remember," asked Cornbread, "when I offered to help you get your grains from Horsefeather's fields? 'There's not much left,' I said. And what did you say?"

"'Nah, I'll do it later,'" Poppy said. "But I was going hiking that day!"

"Don't you remember," asked Cornbread, "when I told you to pick your berries from Grandma Winkle's farm? 'They're almost gone,' I said. And what did you say?"

"'Nah, I'll do it later,'" Poppy said. "But I was playing on my swing set!"

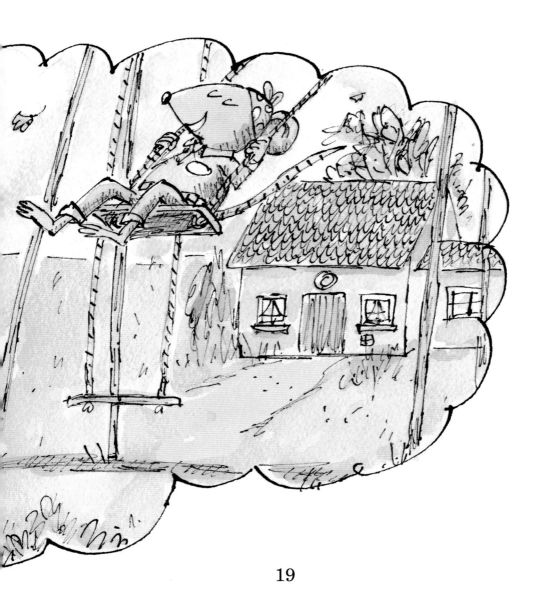

A winter without food is a dangerous thing.

"Oh no, Cornbread!" said Poppy.

"Oh no, Poppy!" said Cornbread.

"Come on, Poppy, let's ask around and see if there's any food left."

Sam was out of cheese.

Horsefeather was
out of grains.

Grandma Winkle was all out of berries.

"Maybe," said Poppy, "one of the neighbors has
extra."

"Shouldn't have waited so long!" said
Old Larry, the town grump.

"What now?" asked Cornbread. He couldn't let his best friend go hungry. "I'll give you some of my food."

"But then you won't have enough to last the winter...," said Poppy. "I don't know what to do."

Poppy looked out the window. She looked out over the town and past the valley, where all the food had already been foraged. Then she looked up at the mountain.

"There might be food...on Holler Mountain," said Poppy.

"No one goes up Holler Mountain!" shrieked
Cornbread.

It was true. No one dared go up Holler
Mountain.

They both look out the window, then up at the mountain.

And they shivered.

❄ Holler Mountain ❄

"There are steep, slippery rocks on Holler Mountain. You could fall!" said Cornbread.

"I know," said Poppy.

"There are owls on Holler Mountain! Owls eat mice!"

"I know," said Poppy.

"Ms. Ruthie went up Holler Mountain to forage for food. She never came back!"

"I know," said Poppy.

It was a sad story. Ms. Ruthie was the only mouse to ever dare go up Holler Mountain. It was years ago, and she was never seen or heard from since. No one ever went up the mountain again.

"It's the only way," said Poppy.

"The only way?" asked Cornbread. Cornbread was worried. And he didn't love adventure like Poppy did. But Poppy was his best friend. And he could not let her go alone. "Then I'm coming with you."

They collected Poppy's wagon and harvesting supplies.

They bundled up in scarves, hats, and jackets. They began their climb up the mountain.

Up, up, up the mountain they went. And so far, so good. There were no owls. But they hadn't found any food yet either. And a heavier snow had now begun to fall.

"Are those blackberry bushes?" Poppy asked.

Strangely, all the berries had been picked.

Up the mountain they went. The snow
continued to fall.

"Are those cornstalks?" asked Cornbread. The
corn was all gone too.

Up the mountain they went. The snow was
getting deeper, and it was getting harder and
harder to climb.

"Is that wheat up there?" asked Poppy.

Just then, a large shadow flew over their path.
They looked up.

"An owl!" they screamed.

They dropped the wagon and ran for the
nearest shrub.

The snow crunch…crunch…crunch…crunched around them. The owl had landed.

Sniff…sniff… "Is that mice I smell?" said a voice.

Cornbread and Poppy shivered. The shrub shivered.

"I like mice!" said the voice.

The shrub shivered.

Poppy grabbed a stone and stood up.

"I'll save you, Cornbread! Run!"

She threw the rock at the owl's toe.

"Ouch! Why'd you do that?" cried the owl.
"I like mice. Mice are my friends."

"We...we thought owls liked to eat mice?"
said Poppy.

"Not me," said the owl.
"I'm a vegetarian."

The large, fluffy, sniffling owl towered over them.

"I'm Bernard," he said.

"I'm sorry, Bernard….I'm Cornbread."

"I'm sorry, Bernard….I'm Poppy."

"What are you doing in the mountain?" asked Bernard. "I don't often see mice up here."

"We were looking for food," said Cornbread.

51

"I know a place with food. Lots of it!" said
Bernard.

Cornbread and Poppy liked the sound of that.

"Can you show us?" asked Poppy, collecting
their wagon.

"I sure can! It's faster if you jump on!" said
Bernard, offering them a ride.

And away they flew.

❄ The Food Problem ❄

A few moments later, they touched down at a small cabin. Smoke was puffing out of a chimney.

"This is my friend's house!" said Bernard.

The cabin door slowly creaked open. An old
mouse came out to greet them.

"Ms. Ruthie! You know Ms. Ruthie?" said
Bernard, Cornbread, and Poppy all at once.

"Cornbread! Poppy! Why, I haven't seen you two in ages!" said Ms. Ruthie. "Come inside and get warm!"

"G'bye, friends!" said Bernard, flapping his great big wings, lifting up and away into Holler Mountain.

"Ms. Ruthie, we thought you were…a goner," said Cornbread.

"I was a goner, all right. I'd gone and moved up here to the mountain. I like being alone!" said Ms. Ruthie. "I'm happy finally to have some mice to keep me company, though! What brings you up here anyway?"

They explained Poppy's food problem.

"Bernard seemed to think you had some food you could share?" asked Poppy sheepishly.

"Oh, do I!" said Ms. Ruthie.

"I've been saving for years! I'm the only mouse who forages up here on Holler Mountain. Take all you want!"

There were jars and jars of berry preserves.

Bags and bags of grain. Hunks and hunks of
cheese.

"But you have to have a cup of Ms. Ruthie's
tea before you go!" their friend said.

It was getting late. Ms. Ruthie helped Cornbread and Poppy load up the food. She even gave them a canister of her special tea leaves to go.

Then she fastened snow skis to their feet and to their wagon for a speedy journey home.

"Thank you so much, Ms. Ruthie!" said Poppy. "You're a real lifesaver! What can I ever do to make it up to you?"

"Just come back and visit sometime!" said Ms. Ruthie.

Cornbread and Poppy zipped
back down the mountain on
the skis.

Naturally, Poppy loved it.

Cornbread was surprised.
He loved it too.

It was quite an adventure.

At Poppy's house, they unloaded and put away all the food.

The snow was very deep. Cornbread helped Poppy shovel her walkway.

They had a cup of Ms. Ruthie's tea to reward themselves for a job well done.

"To old friends," said Poppy.

"Let's ski some more!" said Cornbread.

"Shouldn't we shovel the walkway at your house, Cornbread? It's almost dark."

"Nah, I'll do it later!" he said.